CINDERELLA

Retold and illustrated by

Barbara McClintock

From the Charles Perrault version

Scholastic Press

New York

Once upon a time,

a nobleman lived happily with his sweet and gentle-natured wife and their young daughter. And when his wife died, he took another, who seemed as sweet and gentle as the first.

But no sooner was the wedding over than the new wife revealed herself to be the mean and jealous person she truly was. She couldn't stand the way her new stepdaughter's pleasing demeanor made her own daughters look silly and selfish. That is why she gave her stepdaughter only rags to wear and made her do all the worst chores around the house.

The poor girl swept all the floors . . .

. . . washed and dried and
pressed the laundry . . .

. . . scrubbed the stairs . . .

. . . and cleaned and scoured
every dish, pot, and pan.

At night, she slept on a thin mattress in the dingy attic, while her stepsisters had a lavish bedroom and all the luxuries they wanted. Her stepmother ruled her father with an iron fist, and the poor girl knew he would only scold her if she complained. So she suffered in patient silence.

After a long day, when her chores were done,
the girl sat by the cinders near the fireplace to keep
warm, which is why she was called Cinderella. But
the older stepsister, who was the meaner of the two,
called her Cinderbottom.

Despite everything, Cinderella in her rags was
still a thousand times more beautiful and dear than
her spoiled stepsisters.

One evening, the girls were invited to a grand ball that was being given by the king's son.

The stepsisters were all aflutter about what to wear and how to arrange their hair.

"And what will you wear, Cinderella?" they teased.

Cinderella sighed. "I'm not going," she said, examining her tattered clothing. But she wished to go with all her heart.

The stepsisters asked Cinderella to help them dress and put up their hair, because she could make whatever she arranged look beautiful. But they couldn't resist taunting her.

"Can you imagine Cinderbottom at the ball?" asked the elder.

"They'd have to follow her around with a dustpan while holding their noses!" said the younger one.

Both squealed with laughter. Cinderella resisted an urge to yank their hair. Instead, she patiently made them look as pleasing as possible.

The time came to go to the ball. Cinderella watched as her stepsisters entered their carriage and drove away. Once they were out of sight, she began to cry.

A kind stranger appeared and asked what the matter was.

"I . . . I wish . . ." Cinderella was crying too hard to talk.

But this kindly woman, who was really her fairy godmother, said,
"I know. You wish you could go to the ball!"

"Oh, yes!" said Cinderella.

"Well, then," said her godmother, "let's get busy."

"We'll start with this pumpkin. Now bring me four mice, a rat,
and four lizards."

This did seem a bit odd to Cinderella, but she found four mice
and a rat in a trap, and four lizards behind a garden pot.

The godmother raised her arms and said the magic words:

"FOOMUS BALOOMUS!"

In a flash, the pumpkin grew into a golden carriage, the four mice changed into four handsome gray horses, the lizards became four liverymen dressed in shining emerald green, and the rat turned into a portly coachman with a jaunty mustache.

Cinderella was amazed.

"Now, one more thing," said the godmother with a smile.

All at once, Cinderella's tattered rags vanished, and the most beautiful dress imaginable appeared in their place. A pair of tiny glass slippers graced her feet.

"My dear," her godmother said, "you must be home before midnight, because at the stroke of twelve, everything will turn back to what it was. Don't forget!"

Cinderella thanked her godmother, stepped into her coach, and rode away.

When the prince heard that an unknown princess had arrived, he rushed to
greet her. He gave Cinderella his arm, and together they walked into the ball.
All eyes were on this charming stranger.

The ladies studied her so that they could copy her hair and dress the next day.
Even the king and queen admired her beauty.

The prince asked her to dance. Her astounding grace enchanted everyone. By the time dinner was served, the prince was so smitten that he couldn't eat a bite.

He gave Cinderella a plate of oranges as a gift. She
brought them to her stepsisters and served them with
kindness. They were dumbstruck that this unknown
beauty would pay them any attention at all.

Suddenly, Cinderella saw that it was a quarter to
twelve. She curtsied and quickly left.

When she got home, Cinderella told her godmother all about the ball and how much she wished to go again the next night. Then she heard her stepsisters at the door.

"You were gone so long," she yawned, pretending she'd been sleeping.

"The most beautiful princess came to the ball!" said the younger stepsister.

"And she gave us her oranges!" said the elder.

"I'd love to see her," said Cinderella. "Won't one of you lend me an old dress so that I could go tomorrow?"

"What a joke!" Both stepsisters laughed. "Lend a dress to a filthy Cinderbottom? Ha!"

Cinderella smiled a secret smile.

The next night, the two stepsisters entered the ball, followed by Cinderella, who was dressed even more beautifully than she'd been the night before.

The moment she arrived, the prince was at her side.

They danced all night, chatting with the ease of old, close friends. The time passed sweetly, and so quickly.

Suddenly, Cinderella heard the
clock strike twelve.

She ran as fast as a startled deer,
and as she bounded down the stairs,
one glass slipper fell from her foot.

Outside the palace stood a pumpkin. From beneath it, four mice, four lizards, and a rat scurried away. Cinderella's elegant dress turned back to rags.

The prince ran after her. But all he found was her little sparkling shoe on the stairs. He held it close for the rest of the night, thinking only of the mysterious princess who had run away with his heart.

The next morning, the stepsisters were beside themselves with excitement. The prince had made a proclamation that he would marry the girl who fit the glass slipper. His valet would go to every house to try the slipper on the foot of each young lady in the kingdom.

"Just think!" the older stepsister said. "What if the slipper fits me?"

"Or me?" wondered the younger one.

Soon the prince's valet appeared at the door, holding the little glass slipper on a cushion.

First the elder stepsister tried on the slipper, but without success.

Then the younger stepsister tried, also with no luck.

"May I try?" whispered Cinderella.
"You?" sneered the stepsisters. "What a stupid idea!"

But, to everyone's great astonishment, the slipper fit
Cinderella's foot perfectly.

When Cinderella pulled the matching slipper from her pocket,
the younger stepsister fainted!

The prince was overcome with joy. Within a few days, a great wedding took place. Cinderella and the prince were married. Her father gave her to the groom with great pride. And Cinderella, in her kindness, forgave her stepmother, and found each of her stepsisters a suitable nobleman to wed. They were all terribly sorry about how they had treated her, and everyone lived happily ever after, forever and a day.

To my research assistant, Larson, for all of his excellent help

Cinderella is the Western European version of an ancient folktale that is told in nearly every known culture. The first written record of the tale comes from China in A.D. 850, and some scholars suspect the tale originated in the Middle East even earlier than that. Barbara McClintock based her retelling of *Cinderella* on the seventeenth-century French version by Charles Perrault. Excellent source notes can be found in *The Oxford Companion to Fairy Tales*, edited by Jack Zipes, Oxford University Press, 2000. Special thanks to Karen Van Rossem of the Scholastic Library for her help in researching *Cinderella*'s history.

Copyright © 2005 by Barbara McClintock

ALL RIGHTS RESERVED. Published by Scholastic Press, an imprint of Scholastic Inc., *Publishers since 1920*.

SCHOLASTIC, SCHOLASTIC PRESS, and associated logos are trademarks and/or registered trademarks of Scholastic Inc.

No part of this publication may be reproduced, stored in a retrieval system, or transmitted in any form or by any means, electronic, mechanical, photocopying, recording, or otherwise, without written permission of the publisher. For information regarding permission, write to Scholastic Inc., Attention: Permissions Department, 557 Broadway, New York, NY 10012

LIBRARY OF CONGRESS CATALOGING-IN-PUBLICATION DATA

McClintock, Barbara. Cinderella / retold and illustrated by Barbara McClintock;

[based on the story by Charles Perrault].— 1st ed.   p. cm.

Summary: Although mistreated by her stepmother and stepsisters, Cinderella meets her prince with the help of her fairy godmother.

ISBN 0-439-56145-0 (alk. paper)

[1. Fairy tales. 2. Folklore—France.] I. Perrault, Charles, 1628-1703. Cendrillon. II. Cinderella. English. III. Title.

PZ8.M17295Cin 2005   398.2—dc22   2003024883

10 9 8 7 6 5 4 3 2 1   05 06 07 08 09

Printed in Singapore 46   First edition, October 2005

The artwork was created in pen, India ink, and watercolor on paper.

The text was set in 13-point Windsor. Book design and lettering was by Rich Deas.